For Dave O'Connor,
with many, many thanks. S.G.

An Imprint of Sterling Publishing
387 Park Avenue South
New York, NY 10016

Text copyright © Sally Grindley, 2006.
Illustrations copyright © Susan Varley, 2006.

This 2013 edition published by Sandy Creek.

ISBN 978-1-4351-4756-0

Manufactured in Johor, Malaysia.
Lot #:
2 4 6 8 10 9 7 5 3 1
02/13

Why is the Sky Blue?

And other curious questions about nature

Sally Grindley and Susan Varley

Sandy Creek
NEW YORK

Rabbit and Donkey lived in the same field. Donkey spent his days in the corner nodding his head wisely and chewing on grass.

Rabbit popped up all over the place. His burrow had many openings, and he used them all.

Donkey was very old and knew a lot of things.

"I know why trees lose their leaves, and how spiders spin their webs, and why the sky is blue," he told anyone who would listen.

Rabbit was very young and wanted to learn.

"I want to learn everything there is to learn," said Rabbit.

"I will teach you what I know," said Donkey, "which is a lot."

"Goody," said Rabbit. "Yes, please."

And he jumped and he ran and he rolled and he bounced across the field and back again.

"But I can only teach you if you sit still and listen," said Donkey.

"I will sit still," said Rabbit. "I will sit still and listen."

Donkey began. "I am going to tell you why the sky is blue."

"Goody," said Rabbit. "I really want to know why the sky is blue."

But before Donkey had got very far, Rabbit wanted to know why the earth is brown. And before he had got any further, Rabbit was jumping around the field pointing at yellow flowers and red berries and white butterflies.

Donkey chewed crossly on a piece of grass and waited . . . and waited. When at last he came back, Rabbit said eagerly, "I found out why berries are red. Shall I tell you why?"

"I know already," said Donkey. "And now it is time for my sleep."

"Oh, but I missed why the sky is blue," said Rabbit. "And I really want to know why. Can I come back tomorrow and have another lesson?"

"I can only teach you if you sit still and listen," said Donkey.

"I will sit still," said Rabbit. "I will sit still and I will listen."

"Then tomorrow I will teach you what I know," said Donkey, "which is a lot."

Rabbit leapt in the air in excitement and ran and rolled and bounced all the way home.

The next day, Donkey began again
to tell Rabbit why the sky is blue.
But before Donkey had got very far,
Rabbit wanted to know about the
sun and the moon and the stars. And
before he had got any further, Rabbit
was rushing around pointing at the clouds and the giant foxes
and owls he could see among them.

Donkey chewed angrily on a piece of grass and waited . . .
and waited.

When at last he came back, Rabbit said eagerly, "Sometimes you can see the moon even when the sun is out."

"I know that," said Donkey. "And now it is time for my sleep."

"Oh, but I missed why the sky is blue, again," said Rabbit. "And I really want to know why. Can I come back tomorrow and have another lesson?"

"One last time," said Donkey. "But I can only teach you if you sit still and listen."

"I will sit still," said Rabbit. "I will sit still and listen."

"Then I will teach you what I know," said Donkey, "which is a lot."

Rabbit leapt in the air in excitement . . .

. . . and ran . . .

. . . and rolled . . .

. . . and bounced all the way home.

The next day, Donkey began again
to tell Rabbit why the sky is blue,
but before he had got very far
Rabbit wanted to know why birds
could fly and he couldn't. And before
he had got any further, Rabbit was
running up a slope and leaping off
it making bird noises and flapping
his paws.

Donkey chewed angrily on a piece
of grass and waited . . . and waited.
Rabbit didn't come back.

Donkey settled down for his sleep then looked across the field. He couldn't see Rabbit anywhere. He began to worry.

"He's young," he said to himself. "He might have got into trouble. I'd better go and find him."

He set off slowly across the field. After a few steps he came to a clump of yellow flowers. He looked among them for Rabbit. Rabbit wasn't there, but he watched the bees collecting pollen from the flower heads.

"It sticks to their legs," he said to himself. "I never noticed that before."

Donkey set off again, more quickly this time, and as he trotted along he looked at the sky and saw woolly sheep among the clouds. "It's a long time since I played that game," he smiled to himself.

He came to the top of the slope Rabbit had run down. He looked around to make sure no one was watching, then he began to gallop. When he reached the bottom he galloped on, enjoying the wind tugging at his ears and ruffling his coat. "It's a long time since I felt that feeling," he laughed to himself.

And then he saw Rabbit, sitting quite still in the middle of some bushes.

"Shhh," said Rabbit when he saw Donkey.

"I was worried about you," whispered Donkey. "What are you doing?"

"I'm counting the spots on ladybugs," said Rabbit. "Did you know that some have more spots than others?"

"No," said Donkey, in amazement, "I didn't know that. I know a lot of things but I didn't know that. Let me see."

Rabbit and Donkey looked together. They sat very still and counted spots until Rabbit began to yawn.

"Donkey," said Rabbit, "can you lift me out of here? I'm stuck."

Donkey smiled. "Hang on to my ears then," he said, lowering his head so that Rabbit could reach. He pulled him out and set him on the ground.

"Come," said Donkey, "I'll take you back home. Today you have taught me something new. Tomorrow I will teach you why the sky is blue."

"But I know why the sky is blue," said Rabbit.

"You do?" said Donkey.

"It's because that was the only color left in the paintbox!" cried Rabbit.

Donkey smiled. Donkey laughed. Donkey cheered and kicked his legs in the air. Then he jumped and he ran and he rolled and he bounced, across the field and back again.

"That's the funniest thing I've heard for a long time," said Donkey. "Climb on my back and I'll carry you, but you must sit still."

"Donkey," said Rabbit. "Why *is* the sky blue?"

Donkey began to tell Rabbit about sunlight and the dust in the air, but before he had got very far, Rabbit had fallen asleep.

Donkey smiled to himself.

"Never mind," he said. "It can wait until morning."